PUMPKIN CAT

ANN TURNER   illustrated by AMY JUNE BATES

Hyperion Books for Children
New York

The wind howled. Thunder boomed. The cat skittered sideways into a ditch, but water pounded after her. Racing ahead, the cat found a hollow pipe to hide in. But the water followed her, pushing, pushing, until she was swept away.

The racing stream tugged her this way and that, and then it slowed and left the cat on a wet green lawn. The cat struggled upright, licked her fur feebly, and staggered forward. Ahead was a building. Buildings meant people, and people meant food and warmth.

Wearily, the ginger cat dragged herself to the top
step. But there were no lights, no open doors, no voices
floating out. Her whole body aching, the cat found a
small door in a tall wooden box
and pushed through.
She slept.

"Oh look, it's a cat!" Warm fingers lifted her out of the wooden box. "Did someone return her with a book? Did they think she was due?"

Lisa chuckled, holding the cat close to her body. The cat hung limply, not moving. "Rochelle? Is she all right?"

The other librarian peered at the cat. Softly, she stroked the cat again and again until a purr rumbled under her thumb. "She's all right, Lisa, just tired and hungry, I think. Let's get her inside."

They bustled around, tipping things out of a large basket and lining it with a green sweater. Rochelle ran across the street to the market to buy some kibble.

"Tuna feast, every cat loves tuna feast!" she said, putting it in a dish near the basket. "Come on, library cat, please eat!"

"She needs a name," Rochelle said. "Something to do with Halloween, since it's in a few days. How about Hallow's Eve?" The cat rubbed against the librarian's legs. She wore soft black shoes. They smelled like sheep.

"No," said Lisa. "We can't call her Eve. She's sort of orange— a ginger cat. How about Pumpkin Cat? Yes, I like that."

Rochelle nodded. "Let's call her Pumpkin Cat."

The cat drank some water, nibbled some food,

pawed through some books,

and explored the high, echoing rooms.

It didn't feel like a home, yet. She knew that homes were more than walls and a roof to keep out the rain. But she wasn't quite sure what was missing.

The next day
the door opened
with a bang! "Now,
second graders," said
Rochelle, "come into the
children's room." Some sat on
the floor, some on chairs, and
one on a cushion that—exploded!
"Yowl!" howled Pumpkin Cat and shot
out into the room. A little girl with braids
chirruped to her, "Kitty, come to Charlotte."
The cat paused, turned, and nosed the little girl's
hand. *"Purr,"* said Pumpkin Cat, *"purr."*

The girl smelled like dog bones and fresh air, and her overalls were soft and cozy. Pumpkin Cat curled up on Charlotte's lap and went to sleep. She remembered that this was part of having a home—a warm lap and someone to pet her.

But when the light faded in the sky, the girl with the braids went away, and the library felt huge and echoing. Pumpkin Cat walked around and around the library looking for a friend. She knew the noisy mice in the cellar could never be her friends.

So she curled up to sleep by the stuffed sock monkey in the children's room. His beady eyes gleamed, but he said not one word. He never did. And the wooden sheep that lived in a barn in the corner, they never said a word either.

One day, the librarian who always wore soft black shoes brought
a pumpkin and put it on her desk. It glowed like a bright orange
moon. Pumpkin Cat could hear the sound of children's voices outside,
of feet running across the lawn. She peered out the open door.

There was Charlotte, but everyone looked strange and different.
A boy wore a shiny silver suit. Charlotte wore a black hat that could
not hide her braids, and a long black dress. Others wore wigs and
frightening masks.

The children circled around a big black pot in the middle
of the lawn. They seemed to be fishing for something, but what?
Pumpkin Cat saw a boy bob up with a red apple in his teeth.
It was all so strange and new that she stayed hidden, and watched.

Off to one side children stuck their fingers into a box filled with sawdust. They scrabbled and held coins up to the fading light. "Look, a nickel! Look, a penny!"

Pumpkin Cat came out for a better look. She wanted to be with them, so she pattered down the steps. When she found Charlotte, the ginger cat rubbed shyly against her leg.

"Here you are! I've been looking for you!" the girl cried. "Look, here's your fortune: 'Today you will find your heart's desire.'"

But her voice was too loud, and Pumpkin Cat was afraid.
She skittered off and hid behind a yew. It wasn't until everyone
had gone away and she heard the librarians calling her that she
crept out from under the branches.

Slowly, she went up the stone steps. She paused at the top,
reluctant to go into the huge, echoing rooms with no one to keep
her company but the noisy mice in the cellar.

"What's this, Rochelle?" Lisa said, taking off her carnival mask and crouching by a basket on the top step. "Someone left something here. It's not one of the prizes, is it?"

Rochelle knelt by the basket and pulled off a fuzzy, pink blanket. Underneath was a tiny black kitten, curled up and sleeping. To one side was a small card.

My name is Halloween Cat, and I need a home.
I like to purr, and tuna is my favorite food.
I hear this library likes Cats.

"Well," said Lisa. "That takes nerve!"

Slowly,
   Pumpkin Cat
      edged up to the basket
      and sniffed.
      What a wonderful smell—
      fur, warm breath,
      a hint of tuna,
      and the stuffy coziness
   that comes from
sleeping under blankets.

Gently,
   she grabbed
the back of the kitten's
neck and took her inside.
The kitten swung back and
forth, purring. Pumpkin Cat
placed her in the basket
where she herself always slept.

Carefully,
thoroughly,
she licked her
from nose to tail,
paying special attention
to her ears.

When she was done,
Pumpkin Cat chirruped
and nudged the kitten
toward the kibble dish.
The kitten ate a few bites.
Pumpkin Cat nudged her
toward the water dish
and then the litter pan.

"Well," Rochelle said, smiling. "I guess someone was right. We are a library that likes cats. And you know, Lisa, Pumpkin Cat needs help with the mice in the cellar."

When they locked up the library, Rochelle took one last look. The two cats were curled together in the basket, ginger head next to black head.

Pumpkin Cat purred and stayed awake long enough to feel the small warm body against hers. Later she would tell the kitten about the mice in the cellar, and how foolish the sock monkey was, and how silent the wooden sheep.

But for now, she had finally found what was missing.

To Lisa and Rochelle,
librarians extraordinaire,
lovers of books and cats
—A.T.

To my Punkin'
—A.J.B.

Printed in Singapore
This book is set in Bookman.
The artwork for each picture was prepared using watercolor.

First Edition
1 3 5 7 9 10 8 6 4 2

Reinforced binding

Library of Congress Cataloging-in-Publication Data on file.

ISBN 0-7868-0494-7

Visit www.hyperionchildrensbooks.com